# BLOWHARD
## A Steampunk Fairy Tale

Books and stories by Katina French

The Clockwork Republic Series
Blowhard
Big Teeth
Mirrors & Magic

The Belle Starr Series
Belle Starr: Whiskey on the Rocks
Belle Starr: The Skull Game
Belle Starr: A Pair of Aces *

The Exodus of Jerry B. Johnson
Flashes of Wonder (Collection)

Bitter Cold
(novella in Once Upon a Clockwork Tale)

*Coming Soon

# BLOWHARD

## A Steampunk Fairy Tale

### KATINA FRENCH

Blowhard: A Steampunk Fairy Tale

Published by 3 Fates Press, LLC, 2025 Bell Rd. Morgantown, IN 46160

Cover art by Katina French

ISBN 978-1-940938-08-0

# BLOWHARD

## A Steampunk Fairy Tale

# CHAPTER 1

Elias Hamm stared off at the horizon, his attention focused on what might lay beyond it rather than the three pigs he was supposed to be slopping. The bright afternoon sun failed to warm the icy air. His breath puffed out like smoke filtered through his muffler. It curled over the brim of his weathered brown hat, before disappearing into the clear blue February sky.

Here in Kansas territory, the meeting of earth and sky seemed an endless distance away. Interminable plains surrounded the homestead he shared with his two older brothers, Jeremiah and William. Their new home could not have possibly been more different from the one they'd left in Philadelphia, back East in the Republic of Pennsylvania. In the crowded city, you could hardly walk ten feet without encountering a wall of some sort. He could barely imagine such endless vistas as the prairie offered, back when he was a boy picking stones out of hooves in the stables next to his Pa's farrier shop.

Before moving West, he'd hoped the frontier

might cure the ache for adventure in his gut. It hadn't. His feet still itched to trod new ground, far from hearth and home. The horizon might seem a million miles away, but the responsibilities of the farm fenced him in on every side. The flat, treeless plains could still hide dozens of dangers and deprivations. To keep the farm running required all three brothers working from morning till night. Family duty made a more effective hobble than any in their father's farrier shop. Elias' adventures were over before they'd begun, and the ending left much to be desired. Not that the beginning or middle had been all that exciting, either.

One of the hogs wobbled up towards the trough, shoving Elias' calf with his nose to hurry up with the slop. The hungry pigs had no more use for his dawdling and daydreaming than his eldest brother, Jeremiah. He'd often accused Jeremiah of being pig-headed. Maybe it was the other way around. Maybe the pigs were starting to think like his brother. He snorted a laugh at that idea. Even pigs weren't as stubborn as the oldest Hamm. He'd proven that just a few weeks ago.

A German railroad man, Otto von Rudolph, had come by the homestead. He'd made an offer to buy their land. The railroad's offer wasn't a fortune, but it was a fair price. Elias wished his brothers would have at least considered it. Elias had no interest in fortune; he wanted freedom. He wasn't suited to a farmer's life, any more than he'd been suited to the similarly unexciting life of a farrier. It didn't matter. Jeremiah was having none of it, and William wouldn't directly oppose their eldest brother. Heaven forbid Jeremiah not get his way in an argument, or admit he didn't know everything.

When they'd first arrived, Jeremiah insisted they build a sod house. He said the earthen bricks were the sturdiest material the land had to offer, and it was probably true. But the soddy was always dark, damp, and worse when it rained. Months of being shut up in such a small space together, along with the worms and mice that crept in through the cracks, wore on all three of them. Still, Jeremiah refused to admit how miserable the living conditions had become. He met every complaint with a derisive snort and a dozen reasons why the soddy was a perfectly fine home.

After a brawl that broke their one good chair, William diplomatically announced a previously-unknown hankering to build a wattle-and-daub house. He spoke with excitement about pictures he'd seen in books he'd carted out from back East, of houses built with sticks and mud. If they could build a house with nothing but twigs and dirt in the Old World, why couldn't they do it here? Elias suspected William's proclamation had more to do with his tendency to play peacemaker than any real enthusiasm about centuries-old building techniques.

Still, he'd jumped at the chance to be out of the sod house. It was also a sweet relief to do something more interesting than monotonous chores. They'd spent days in the nearest river bed, gathering wagon loads of saplings, reeds, rushes and buckets of mud.

Building William's cottage was one of the few happy times they'd enjoyed since coming out West. Splashing around in the creek bed, Elias managed to surprise Jeremiah with a mud ball to the face. After a second of shocked indignation, Jeremiah grabbed up a handful of muck and slung it back at him.

They'd played like boys again, flinging mud and having a refreshing swim in the deepest part of the river. For just a day, life wasn't all work. Then they finished the round cottage, and the arguments began anew.

Jeremiah refused to leave the soddy. Before long, he complained the wattle-and-daub house was a waste of time and materials. William tried to smooth things over.

"You're the oldest, Jeremiah." he'd said "You deserve a house of your own!"

Elias even joined in teasing, "If you're lonely, you'd best get busy finding a wife."

But it was clear the gruff eldest Hamm was offended, wanderlust still afflicted the youngest, and try as he might, nothing the middle brother could do would reconcile them.

A few months later, William suggested they build a house for Elias. Maybe he'd hoped a place of his own would settle him down. Maybe it was another attempt to convince Jeremiah they hadn't deserted him.

"More settlers are arriving in Kansas territory every day. It won't be long now before we've got enough folk to declare ourselves an independent republic, just like Arkansas, New Africa, or the Free Sioux Nation," William had reasoned. "The more people who come, the more land disputes we'll see. We don't want a situation like the James boys dealt with last month. If we've got three houses on the property, they'd be almost like guard posts. If you count the barn, that's four buildings standing on our claim. Might make it seem like we're more of a fight than most would want to take on."

Appealing to Jeremiah's pessimism was usually a good strategy, and it had worked. As for

Elias, he'd do anything William asked.

He'd tried to get excited about the house. They'd built it out of straw bales covered in the same clay adobe mixture they'd used on William's cottage. There weren't enough saplings or reeds left in the creek bed for another wattle-and-daub house. Another soddy was out of the question. Elias had sneered "Even the livestock hate their sod barn."

Since he'd moved into the straw bale house, there'd been fewer fights between he and Jeremiah. A fine house, it ended up by far the nicest of the three they'd built. It boasted waxed paper in the windows, and a thatched roof the old Irishman from a nearby claim helped them build. It was so fine, William had started pestering Jeremiah to build one for himself. Neither Elias nor William could figure why Jeremiah refused to leave that filthy old soddy.

Of course, Jeremiah's pride would stand for no such thing.

"You know about the wind storms they have out in this country? Twisters, they call 'em. First time one passes this way, you two will be lamenting all your hard work gone, and I'll be snug in my soddy. Maybe then you'll listen to me."

Elias snickered at that thought. They'd been here nearly four years, and had not seen a single one of these twisters Jeremiah went on about. The old timers spoke of them with awe. Maybe they were just a tall tale concocted by the local tribes, or earlier settlers, to keep people from moving out to stake a claim. Even if they were real, with so much land, the odds of one crossing their tiny farm seemed remote. Certainly not odds worth living in a house as cold and moldy as the grave.

He looked up from the hog trough after another impatient nudge from the pig. It was much darker than it should have been for this time of day. A bank of black clouds moved swiftly across the sky. A thick fog rolled in, making it impossible to see more than a few feet in any direction. A hard rain pelted his hat and coat. Icy wind slapped his face and numbed his hands, which still clutched the slop bucket. The pig snorted and trotted off in the direction of the barn.

"That was awful sudden." Later in the year, storms could come up quick like this, exploding in the summer heat like popcorn over the fire. *Might odd weather for February*, he thought.

A sound like the trains back East roared behind him, just over the nearest prairie swell. Elias turned. His muffler whipped around him, lashing his face. Sheer terror gripped him as he spotted a great whirling cloud rushing towards him. It looked like a spool of dirty grey wool, spinning upwards on a spindle that reached the heavens. He dropped the slop bucket, but it never hit the ground. The wind snatched it away before plucking him off his feet. It spun him around as if he weighed no more than a stalk of wheat. It held him aloft for a long moment, sucking the breath from his burning lungs. One of the pigs sailed through the air past him, squealing in panic, its legs flailing.

The next thing he knew, he shot backwards like a cannonball, landing in the frigid wet pig trough. He struggled to get up, but the wind still blew in a high gale. Bits of straw filled the air, along with much fouler debris from the pig pen. The wooden slop bucket he'd dropped in surprise sailed back at him, mercifully empty. It slammed into his head with stunning force. He fell backwards again, his head resting against the lip of the trough. His vision filled with blurry red, then grey, and finally black.

# CHAPTER 2

"William! I've found him!"

Jeremiah's voice rang through Elias' head like the peal of a brass church bell on Sunday morning after drinking cheap whiskey Saturday night.

Elias blinked his eyes open to discover both his brothers leaning over him, worried looks etched on their faces.

"Help me get him out of this thing," said Jeremiah, "We'll be lucky if he doesn't die of frostbite." Soon their thickly gloved hands were wrapped around his shoulders and knees, tugging him out of the pig trough.

"What happened?" he asked, groaning.

"The same thing I've been telling you fools would happen sooner or later. A twister. Came up out of the south and blew right across the farm. William and I saw it and came running."

William looked at him sadly. "It took your house, Elias. I'm sorry."

"What do you mean, it took my house?"

"The twister just blew it to bits. There's nothing left but piles of straw and pieces of busted adobe. Your clothes, the bedstead and quilts, the table — it's all flung hither and yon."

"The pigs?"

Jeremiah shook his head, glancing over his shoulder. "Looks like one of them is dead. Neck's broken. Not sure how that happened."

Elias was pretty sure he knew, but telling his brothers he'd actually seen a pig fly seemed like a quick way to get himself sent back East to Greystone Asylum.

They'd managed to get him mostly upright. He was a little dizzy, and he felt bruised and beaten. No worse than after a particularly rough brawl with Jeremiah. Nothing seemed to be broken, at least. He was soaked to the skin, freezing cold, and his teeth chattered so hard he was afraid they might break. He looked up into a clear winter sky. The thick clouds had disappeared along with the wind and rain, although he could see that peculiar fog bank rolling off a mile or more away.

It was all too strange. The old timers agreed the only good thing about a Kansas winter was the absence of twisters. Even in the summer, storms could seem to come out of nowhere, but you could still see the clouds receding into the distance. He wondered what on earth happened to cause this freak storm.

# CHAPTER 3

Otto von Rudolph cackled like an old chicken. He rolled with hilarity from one side of the luxurious red velvet sofa to the other, as the curious steam carriage chugged away from the Hamm's property. The buttons on his brocade waistcoat strained at the pressure of containing his bulging gut as it shook with laughter. His polished boots beat the floor in gleeful excitement.

"It worked, my dear girl! It worked! Did you see the hog? As God is my witness, even if I didn't need those fool boys' land, it would have been worth the effort just to see a pig fly!"

At the steering wheel of the carriage, Mathilde "Mattie" Amsel didn't think it was all that funny. She'd been appalled when she'd spotted living creatures, including a man, through her spyglass. Guilt gripped her heart when she'd realized they were right in the path of their machine-made tornado. She'd winced at the loud crack of the poor pig's neck as the winds slammed it into the ground after whirling the terrified beast in circles.

She hoped the man their storm had tossed

into the pig trough had survived. Otherwise, she was guilty of murder. If that were the case, the tight leash Uncle Otto had around her neck could quickly become a noose if she stepped out of line. She could hardly bear it, even before now.

Why, she wondered for the thousandth time, had her parents decided to leave Bavaria for the New World? Both her parents were struck ill during the long sea voyage. Neither had ever recovered, dying within days of each other only weeks after arriving in the Republic of New York. Mattie had been taken in by her uncle Otto, who'd emigrated with his grandparents as a child.

At the time, she'd been grateful. Now she wished he'd sent her back to Bavaria.

Mattie adjusted her driving goggles under the earflaps of her shearling cap, and pulled her muffler up around her neck. Her straw-blond hair was braided and coiled into a knot. It provided no protection against the cold. The fog that swirled around the steam carriage as camouflage gradually dissipated. The curious conveyance was more comfortable than a traditional horse-drawn carriage would have been over such rough terrain. She'd worked hard on the springs and coils in its suspension to ensure that much. Unlike a locomotive, it could travel anywhere without need for tracks. But the open cockpit was still miserably cold, far from the boiler in the back which powered its steam-driven engine.

The boiler also powered the Wind Oscillating Lift Field Engine, or W.O.L.F.E., which was her uncle's idea but unfortunately her own creation. She may have created it under duress, but she was still responsible for the destruction it wrought. She should have just refused to do as Uncle Otto had asked. She should have pretended to be incapable of creating such a device, no matter how dire the consequences of failure had seemed. Now, it was too late. The machine had worked, all too perfectly. There was no going back.

After the events of today, there was no denying her uncle was not simply an egotistical, lazy old braggart. He was a ruthless, murderous thief. No one with a scrap of conscience could have turned on the machine even after Mattie had screamed there was a man in the path of the storm. The young man had been too far away to hear her warning, but Uncle Otto had heard her clearly enough. He'd glared at her and thrown the switch, every bit the monster she'd long suspected.

She'd tried to learn to like him when she'd first come to live with him. She knew she should be grateful he'd taken her in, instead of letting her go to an orphanage. Despite her best intentions,

Otto's interminable lectures and endless gloating had soured her disposition towards him. For all his boasting, he was really only a cog in the railroad company machine. She doubted even the company's owners knew exactly how far their cog would go in pursuit of his own ambition.

Her uncle's work meant they were always moving from place to place. They weren't rich, but Otto's salary provided them with a relatively luxurious life. They traveled for free, ate in the dining car for free, and never paid rent. The railroad maintained company boarding houses in most of the republics and territories. Some of them were quite large and impressive. Otto and Mattie moved from one to the other as her uncle's work had demanded.

Her favorite places were cities where other families had boarded in the railroad house, but she never remained long enough to make friends. After ten years of constant travel, Mattie wanted more than anything to settle down somewhere pleasant, and never leave. In her dreams, she would move to a port city, and let the world come to her for a change.

No matter how hard she tried, she couldn't quite bring herself to love her uncle. It was more than his off-putting personality. There was something about him that just wasn't quite right.

Mattie had always enjoyed taking things apart and putting them back together. As a young child, she'd occupied her time building small devices from spare parts left lying around the railroad boarding houses. Most were simple, but a few were quite ingenious. By the time she was ten, she could fix almost anything broken around the house, given a few parts, some time and some basic tools.

When he discovered her talent for mechanical work, Otto gave her free reign in the railroad garages. At first, she was delighted. However, she soon learned that for every hour she got to work on her own inventions, Otto expected her to spend a dozen doing tedious maintenance work for the railroad. From the time she was twelve, Mattie had kept some of the railroad's oldest and most worn-out steam engines running.

On better days, she worked on building labor-saving devices. Not that Uncle Otto was ever up to much labor worth saving. She built simple clockwork automatons capable of performing a single repetitive task. One could wash a load of laundry and wring it nearly dry. One of the more complicated devices could toast a piece of bread, cut a circle from the center, drop it into a hot skillet and crack an egg into the hole for breakfast. As long as you remembered to butter the skillet, the results were delightful.

She lacked the knowledge of alchemy required to build 'gens, mechanical servants capable of following simple commands. Still, up until now, she'd been proud of every machine she'd created. Alchemists meddled in forces no one really understood. The railroads might like alchemical coal since it burned longer. In Mattie's opinion, you didn't need a magic potion to power a machine that buttered your toast or washed your unmentionables.

She had often thought about leaving Uncle Otto. With her mechanical skills, surely she could make her own way in the world. By the time she was fourteen, Mattie had started planning to escape her uncle's grip once she was of legal age.

Unfortunately, Uncle Otto had no intention of letting such a valuable asset go free. The summer of her fifteenth year, he'd taken her on a short trip back East. It had almost been pleasant, except for the brief visit to Crimpworth's Home for Wayward Girls. It was a filthy workhouse filled with half-starved, dead-eyed girls, all of whom were clearly being driven to an early grave.

He'd patted her shoulder, gesturing at the rows of scrawny, underfed wretches. "We're here to take pity upon these poor girls — who must have been terribly disobedient to end up in such a place! —and make a donation to their care."

But Mattie saw no money leave her uncle's pudgy hands. His real meaning, and the implied threat, was unmistakable.

Mattie would prefer he tied her up and left her on one of his cursed railroad tracks than send her to that abominable place. So she'd kept her mouth shut, at least when he was in earshot. She'd done what he'd told her when she couldn't figure out a way to undo it without getting caught. These last months, her skills at sabotage had gotten nearly as good as her ability to create and repair. She'd snuck into marketplaces and sold the smallest of her devices whenever she could get away. Her one hope was to hide enough money to escape and start a tinker shop of her own. Unfortunately, Uncle Otto kept finding her secret hiding places, emptying them of her hard-earned savings without a word passed between them.

Then this month, just after they'd come to Kansas, he'd informed her of his secret project. He needed a device capable of clearing a swath of ground for a mile in any one direction. After hearing tales of the local storms, he'd demanded she build a machine that could create a small, temporary cyclone. He said it was to help the railroad clear ground in overgrown parts of the country, without the need to hire so much unskilled labor. It had seemed like a foolhardy and grandiose solution to a simple problem, but foolish and grandiose was completely in character for her uncle.

She'd had an inkling of the machine's true purpose, but she also had no doubt refusing to build it would've sent her to Crimpworth's faster than Otto could gobble down a plate of schniztel.

The W.O.L.F.E. had taken up most of her time, and Otto had cordoned off the local railroad garage from any other workers or maintenance jobs. When the machine was complete, he'd been forced to confess his real purpose. He wanted to use it to drive intractable homesteaders off property the railroad needed to run a new line from *le Republique de Louisiane* to the Pacific coast.

He'd huffed and puffed at her objections. He'd claimed the young men who owned the Hamm claim were nowhere near the straw bale building at this time of day. He'd talked of watching their daily habits. He'd promised her they were all in the sod house together, perfectly safe. He'd assured her that the Hamm brothers would be better off taking his money and moving somewhere more hospitable than the Kansas plains. He'd blustered that he was doing them a charity, but she believed none of it. Now, the events of the day had proven her skepticism sterling true. If only she'd been able to escape him sooner. If only she'd had the courage to refuse to build it, regardless of the consequences. Now she was trapped, probably a murderer and unable to call the authorities on her uncle without implicating herself equally. Perhaps she deserved to be stuck with him.

Then she considered what *else* he might ask her to build someday. A chill ran down her spine which had nothing to do with the cold Kansas wind.

As her mad uncle laughed, yammering on about his triumphant success, she knew the time had come. She couldn't bear the thought of being responsible for someone else getting hurt or killed just for standing in the way of Otto's boundless ambition. She needed a plan to get out from under this blowhard's thumb, and she needed it fast.

It was a good thing Mattie absolutely excelled at devising clever plans. She had a whole room full of blueprints and sketches to prove it.

# CHAPTER 4

"I think we should consider that German fella's offer." Elias' voice sounded deeper and raspier after having most of the air ripped out of his throat. If it could only give his words more weight with his brother, he'd have considered it a small price to pay.

"Well, that's why we don't trust you to do the thinking around here." Jeremiah didn't even bother to look up from the bowl of stew he was shoveling down when Elias had stormed into the soddy.

He'd come to see if Jeremiah might budge on selling the claim. In hindsight, maybe he should have asked William to come along as well. Maybe they could have persuaded him together. The only problem was, Elias couldn't tell how his diplomatic middle brother really felt about leaving Kansas and giving up on the farm. Ferreting out William's true opinion was like digging for gold, especially on any topic under contention. Will would probably rather walk across a harvested wheat field barefoot than pick sides between his brothers.

As for Jeremiah, his opinion was as painfully clear as it was unchangeable.

"No, of course not," Elias yelled. "Nobody's allowed to have a thought in his head you didn't approve of first!"

"You can be sure I never approved of that blasted straw bale house! Biggest fool notion I ever heard of. If you and Will had just been willing to stay here in the soddy with me a couple more years, we could have—"

"We could have taken each other's heads off! That's what we could've done. We were all sick of living in this disgusting hole, Jeremiah! He might not have ever said it out loud, but Will was just as tired of being buried here with you and the field mice as I was! The place doesn't hold enough air for anyone else to breathe, so long as it's filled with an insufferable, overbearing know-it-all blowhard like you!"

The look of shock on his brother's face made Elias immediately regret his words. It was true, but he knew from years of Jeremiah's stinging words how painful the truth could be when delivered without grace or kindness.

"Jeremiah. . . ."

"Get out. You've said your piece. I won't make you suffer my insufferable company." Jeremiah tucked back into the stew. Elias had seen miners swing a pickaxe with less force than his brother was expending on scooping meat and vegetables up out of his bowl.

Elias opened his mouth to speak, and then closed it. Anything he said now would probably only make things worse.

He opened the door to the soddy. A sound carried over the field, making a chill run down his spine to his very toes. It sounded like a train bearing down the railroad tracks. The sky was black and roiling to the west — right in the direction of the wattle-and-daub cottage. He turned, but Jeremiah had already rushed to the door.

"William!" he bellowed, shoving Elias out of the way as he barreled towards the field separating the soddy from Will's cottage.

Elias ran after him, his face bleached pale with fear. The cottage was a good distance away. By the time he and Jeremiah arrived, the twister had already come and gone. Its devastation was still clear. The little wattle-and-daub house was gone, with only a pile of debris left in its place. Jeremiah ran to the wreckage, calling Will's name.

Elias spotted something out of the corner of his eye. A dark shape just over the next rise, surrounded by a cloud of fog. It moved away at a fast but steady pace. A fat curl of steam poured out a pipe at the back of it. He ran towards it. In just a moment, he had climbed to the top of the sod barn, looking down on a bizarre, fog-cloaked steam carriage.

A small figure in a shearling cap and goggles, wrapped in a heavy coat, with dark britches and heavy boots steered it by means of what looked like a ship's wheel. The bundled figure's boots pressed levers on the floorboards of the machine. A gloved hand occasionally twisted a knob on a long pole. Behind the driver, through the carriage window, he spied a figure he was almost certain was the German railroad man, Von Rudolph. As the fog cleared, he could see the back of the carriage held a boiler. An engine made up of a twisted conglomeration of different pumps, wheels, gears, and spiraling fans was bolted to the back.

He started to run after the steam carriage, but a cry from Jeremiah stopped him in his tracks. He turned back and ran to the ruined cottage. His eldest brother was kneeling over a pile of broken and twisted pieces of wood. He could barely see a hand, limp and poking out of the bottom. The hand didn't move.

He dropped to his knees beside Jeremiah and clawed desperately at the wreckage that buried their beloved brother. When they found his face, it was pale and battered, his eyes closed. Jeremiah yanked off his glove. He placed his hand over Will's mouth and nose.

"Thank God. He's breathing. Let's get him out of here." They spent the next several minutes excavating him from the rubble of his home. It was clear he was in bad shape, but he was still alive.

Elias found a piece of woven wall still intact. "Jeremiah, we can use this as a travois to get him back to the soddy."

"Good idea." Jeremiah cleared the rest of the debris off Will and helped Elias slide the piece of wall beneath him.

Elias had waited his whole life to hear his brother say those words to him. Now, he just hoped his idea was good enough idea to get Will to safety.

&#x273B;*&#x273B;

William was sleeping on a pallet at the back of the soddy. They'd discovered his leg was broken as soon as they'd gotten him inside. He'd passed out from the pain while they set and splinted it. Once their brother was as comfortable as they could make him, Elias told Jeremiah what he'd seen: the steam carriage with Von Rudolph inside, and the curious device on the back.

"Jeremiah, have you ever heard of one cyclone during this time of year? Much less two hitting the same farm in less than a week's time?"

"No. And I've never heard of a storm coming out of a clear blue sky and disappearing this fast. As crazy as it sounds, that railroad man might've found a way to bottle a twister."

"More like uncork the bottle."

Jeremiah nodded solemnly. "If he's got that kind of power, I reckon we don't have much choice. We'll have to take his offer for the claim. I just hope he's willing to wait till Will's well enough to travel."

Elias saw his brother's shoulders slump in defeat. Maybe Kansas hadn't turned out to be the grand adventure he'd been seeking all his life. It didn't mean it wasn't the fulfillment of his brothers' dreams. Rage boiled up inside him. No one was going to take it away from them. Not if Elias had anything to say about it.

"No, we don't have to take his offer. How *can* we, knowing he might have done this to William? I'm getting to the bottom of this, Jeremiah. If he's responsible, he's gonna pay for his crimes." He stood up from the stool at the table, reaching for his coat and hat.

"No." Jeremiah's voice was colder and heavier than lead.

"Jeremiah, now is not the time to tell me how foolhardy and useless I am." He glared at his older brother, who still sat with his head in his hands.

"You're not foolish, El." Jeremiah looked up and sighed. "You're brave. You always were. So brave you scared me, Ma, Papa and Will half to death from the time you could walk. And you're not useless. We need you here, especially with Will in this shape. I should be the one to go. I'm the oldest. Better yet, we should wait and go together. This fella could be dangerous."

"Jeremiah, somebody's going to have to take care of William right now. You know you're the best man for that job. You've been taking care of us all our whole lives. I don't know if he saw me or not. If we wait, he could hide that infernal contraption — or worse, use it again. I'll be careful. If it looks like a bad deal, I'll just pretend I'm there to take him up on his offer."

"Is there anything I can do to stop you from going?" Jeremiah looked like he'd aged ten years in the last ten hours. Elias hated to put one more worry on his shoulders, but if the railroad man was behind this, they needed to end it.

Elias shook his head. "You're not going to leave Will and you're not going to shoot me to keep me here. So, no, you can't stop me. I'm going whether you agree to it or not."

"Then go, and take the rifle. And if you find out he did this? Put that devil in the ground. Or at least, leave him in worse shape than our boy here."

# CHAPTER 5

One of the Hamm brothers was at the front door. Mattie was certain of it. Now, this was an interesting turn of events. She'd been formulating her plan of escape, lining up the different pieces like the cogs of a great machine. Depending on this young man's intentions and actions, she might need to set her machinations in motion, adjust the blueprint, or throw out the plans and invent something new on the fly.

She sucked in a breath. This was her chance to find out if his brother was still alive. Her relief at finding out the first young man had survived his encounter mostly unharmed had felt like a boxcar was lifted off her chest. The relief soon dissipated, though. It only took a few days for her uncle to decide to destroy a second house. The Hamms had refused his second offer for their land. She'd begged him to wait, let them catch their breath from the first storm. She tried reasoning with him, telling him that two freak storms hitting a single farm barely a week apart would raise suspicions. He'd only laughed.

"Who do you suppose would suspect we've built a machine that can launch a cyclone? No, my dear. Trust me. These homesteaders would sooner believe they're the victims of terrible luck. The first storm only has them digging in their heels. This one will convince them that Kansas is cursed ground for them. You will see."

This time, she'd refused to operate the W.O.L.F.E., claiming that she saw a broken gear that needed to be replaced. Much to her chagrin, her uncle had paid close attention earlier and started the machine himself, ignoring her warning. She'd driven the carriage, not daring to defy him more directly. But at least it'd been Otto himself who'd started and run the W.O.L.F.E., without her help.

She'd prayed all three men were in the soddy when he had launched the cyclone at the odd round house. But she'd only two ran out of the sod house when the storm roared through the field. She could have sworn she'd seen one of them climb the roof of their barn and stare after them as they rattled away. Could it be possible? Could someone else have figured out her uncle's insane scheme already? For all she knew, the man had already contacted the local sheriff. Although Otto was probably right. He'd have quite a time convincing any sane man her uncle had a cyclone machine tucked into one of the railroad's garages.

The truth was sometimes the hardest thing for people to believe.

Mattie slipped into the front parlor. Uncle always met with visitors in there. She had just enough time to hide behind the heavy drapes. She thanked heaven for the time it would take her portly uncle to amble down from his room and answer the door. The thick velvet drapes were so dusty she almost sneezed as she slipped behind them. It reminded her of plans she'd drawn for a device to clean carpets and drapes, based on a suction pump. Unfortunately, all the parts she could get her hands on lately had gone into that blasted W.O.L.F.E.

Moments later, her uncle ushered a man she recognized as Elias, the youngest of the Hamm brothers, into the parlor. He was dressed in a long coat, a broad-brimmed hat pulled low over shaggy dark hair. A rifle hung over his shoulder, but Otto's jovial tone didn't sound as though he'd come looking for vengeance. Mattie hoped it meant no one had paid for her uncle's folly with his life. Yet.

"I'm so pleased to hear your brothers have made the sensible decision at last," Otto intoned. "This barren land is a dreadful place. Your misfortune with these cyclones is surprising for this time of year, but it's hardly uncommon for settlers to meet a bad end. You're far better off returning to your home in, Philadelphia, was it? And just think of all the people the new railway line will benefit!"

"Funny you should mention how rare it is to see a twister in winter, Mr. Von Rudolph. Seems nobody ever heard of *one* happening this time of year. Nobody's ever heard of two hitting the same piece of property so quick, either." Behind the curtain, Mattie heard her uncle fussing with papers in his desk. After a short pause, Elias continued.

"Another funny thing? You said *cyclones*, not cyclone. A second twister *did* come through earlier today. Only we haven't told a soul about it, and I didn't mention it when I said I wanted to talk about your offer." Mattie held her breath. The young man may not have implied Otto was responsible for the storms, but he certainly seemed suspicious of *something*.

"Well, it's a small town, son. I suppose I heard it from one of your neighbors who happened by and saw the storm."

Mattie furrowed her brow in consternation. Otto sounded altogether too calm. She knew that calm, and it was dangerous. The young man replied to her uncle with steel in his voice.

"Oh, I saw someone passing by. But it wasn't any neighbor I know. Strangest thing I ever saw. A steam carriage with a boiler and some infernal-looking contraption mounted to the back. Had a bunch of pumps and fans, big ones. Reckon they could stir up an awful lot of wind."

"You don't say, my boy? Well, I've certainly never seen or heard of any such machine here in town."

"Really, Mr. Von Rudolph? Because I could have sworn I saw *you* through the window."

Mattie sucked in a breath.

"What precisely are you trying to say, boy? I thought you said you'd come here to make a deal."

"I did, and here's the deal. You take me to the carriage house out back. Let me go through that old railroad garage on the other side of town. Convince me it wasn't your steam carriage, and we'll take your offer. We'll sell you the claim and leave Kansas."

"What of your brothers? Were either of them lost in the storm?" For a moment, Mattie thought perhaps her uncle was showing a glimmer of humanity, but his next words made it clear he was all business. "How can I take the word of the youngest, who may have no legal right to sell? Your oldest brother seemed quite determined to stay on the claim."

"My brothers are both alive, though William has a broken leg." Mattie exhaled a soft sigh of relief. She was not a murderer, at least not yet. The young man went on. "I've spoken with Jeremiah, the oldest of us. He's agreed to follow my advice."

"Very well, young Mr. Hamm. We'll take a quick tour of the carriage house and garage. When you're satisfied I have nothing to do with this mysterious steam carriage of yours, we'll settle our business."

From behind the curtain, Mattie's brow furrowed. She had expected her uncle to insist that the very idea of a cyclone machine was ridiculous. She'd expected him to give a dozen reasons why he couldn't give the man access to official railroad property, or at the very least try to delay any such inspection. The steam carriage was locked away in the garage workshop. There was nowhere else to hide such a thing. When they arrived in the garage, Uncle Otto's lies would be obvious. What was he playing at?

She heard the two men leave the room, headed towards the carriage house. If she were quick, she could slip out the back and sneak over to the garage. She could be hidden again before they got there.

She bolted through the kitchen door and out into the alley behind the boarding house. She managed to scramble down the alley without raising the attention of anyone but a few cackling hens behind the dry goods store. Her sturdy work boots kicked up a cloud of dust, but it would have a few minutes to settle before Elias and Uncle Otto arrived.

Mattie clambered up a rickety ladder onto a haphazard wooden storage shelf that covered half the garage. She tucked herself under a tarp next to a crate someone had pulled close to the edge. It provided a good vantage point, with very little chance of discovery. Even if they were directly below her, she could peep through the wide gaps between the wooden planks under her feet.

The waiting set her nerves on edge. Just when she thought maybe they weren't coming, the garage doors slid open and both men entered.

She heard her uncle ask Elias to go light the oil lantern, since it was getting dark. There was a huge, glowing coal furnace near the back of the garage, to run the forge and power some of the tools. But there were no windows and with all the machines and tools scattered throughout the space, it offered little illumination. Elias lit the lantern. When the light flared, it clearly revealed the dark hulking mass in the back of the workshop. The steam carriage wasn't even covered with a canvas or tarpaulin. As Elias lifted the lantern and turned towards her uncle, the garage door slid shut with a loud clang.

Highlighted in the lantern's glow against the inky backdrop of the door, her uncle pulled out a revolver. He pointed it at young Mr. Hamm's chest.

"Now, we will arrange a new deal, Mr. Hamm. And this time, I will be dictating the terms."

# CHAPTER 6

Elias stared down the barrel of Von Rudolph's six-shooter, wishing he'd just taken Jeremiah's advice for once.

He'd brought the rifle, but instead of keeping it in hand the whole time, he'd hung it across his back. He'd worried about attracting the attention of the sheriff stalking through town with a gun in hand. It seemed like a bad idea when you were on a mission of possibly lethal vengeance. Besides, Von Rudolph had seemed like such a weak, dandified bureaucrat. He'd figured any fighting the railroad man needed doing was performed by a hired gun. He'd let himself get taken off guard, and now it didn't matter if the old windbag was a decent shot or not. If Elias reached for the rifle, Otto couldn't possibly miss at this range.

Whatever he'd said before coming, Elias had hoped it wouldn't come down to killing. He'd figured his meaty fists, and years of brawling with his brothers, would be enough to make Otto regret putting his family in harm's way. He'd imagined beating the man senseless, and then destroying the infernal twister machine.

Now he was in a sorry fix. The pudgy old man had hoodwinked him. He was used to getting into scrapes; he wasn't used to getting out of them without any help from his brothers. It was entirely up to him to figure out a way out of this mess.

If he wasn't likely about to get himself shot, it would've been the greatest moment of his life. He'd wanted excitement and adventure. It looked like he was going to get more than he'd bargained for.

"Alright, you got the jump on me, Von Rudolph. I can see your blasted twister machine in the corner. You planning on shooting me right here in town? I reckon even you'd have a hard time talking your way out of that. I saw the sheriff and a half-dozen townsfolk within shouting distance. Judging by the miserable offer you made for our land, I doubt you could come up with enough cash to bribe your way out of the hangman's noose."

"Rest assured, if I had to shoot you here and now, I could and would. You don't think I could kick your worthless carcass under one of these tarps? Anyone who came running, I'd just tell them I'd heard a strange noise, and misfired my pistol when I came in here to investigate."

Elias tensed a bit at that, but he figured as long as he kept him talking, he stood a chance of getting away.

"So why haven't you shot me already?"

"I'd prefer not to be that obvious. A man of my position has to make sure there's no chance of being implicated in any such sordid dealings. I can assure you, the railroad doesn't care what I do to accomplish my ends, but at the first whiff of scandal they'll throw me to the wolves. Why do you think I resorted to something as outlandish as this ridiculous machine to get you off your claim? Who could possibly believe I'd engineered a cyclone?" He nodded in the direction of the steam carriage.

"No, I'm not going to shoot you just yet, unless you make me. There are better ways to get rid of an enemy. Especially one known for getting into violent arguments with his brothers." Von Rudolph smiled. It was not a pleasant expression. "I think you are all about to have just such an argument this evening. Tragically, you'll end up killing each other in a drunken rage, most likely disputing whether to sell your worthless claim. It's a bit messier than my original plan, but it will have to suffice."

Elias felt all the color drain from his face, as he wondered what kind of madman thought blowing away someone's home with a whirlwind was less messy than a bullet to the chest.

"Seems like you've got this all thought out," said Elias, still stalling for time. Maybe if he convinced Von Rudolph he wasn't going to put up any resistance, he could wrestle the gun from him on the way back to the homestead.

"Indeed. Your corn-fed brawn might give you the advantage if I were foolish enough to let you get within arm's reach, but you are no match for my superior wit. I know you'll try to attack me the minute my back is turned. That is why you'll be getting into that storage cabinet behind you. My niece designed it to lock as soon as the doors close." He gestured to a heavy, ornate brass and steel cabinet with a door that was at least three inches thick.

Elias felt like a cornered animal who'd heard the cage door clank shut an instant after he'd backed into it. Why did he have to be so pig-headed? Jeremiah had tried to tell him to wait until they could go together, but he'd been hell-bent to get to the bottom of things right that minute.

"Now kindly grab your rifle, by the barrel, and lay it on the ground."

Since it was do as he was told, or take a bullet at point blank range, he dropped his gun. Von Rudolph waved him towards the cabinet.

He stepped into it.

"Kindly shut the door, Mr. Hamm." Elias glared at him, but did as he was told. He heard the whirring of gears and the sound of tumblers falling into place. He heard the older man pick up his rifle.

"I shall have to leave you for a few moments, my boy. Getting that cabinet loaded onto a wagon will require the crane, so I'll need my niece's assistance."

He heard the door slide open and closed again. The cabinet was too narrow and shallow to allow him much movement, even if it hadn't been crowded with repair parts and tools. It was built like a coffin and dark as a tomb, which was appropriate since he'd most likely die in it. He had seen a set of tools hung from hooks on the side of the cabinet before the door had shut out every bit of light. He felt for a wrench, and started beating at the cabinet door, albeit with very short swings.

"Stop that! You're going to ruin my locking mechanism and then I'll never get you out of there!" A woman's voice, muffled by metal and tinged with a faint German accent, called out to him.

"Who's out there?" he yelled.

"Be quiet!" the hushed voice snapped. "The

last thing we need is for my uncle to hear your racket and come back. We've little enough time as it is."

He heard the rattle of a key ring. A moment later, the thick iron door swung open. A dainty young woman in her late teens stood before him, holding the lantern and glaring at him with steel gray eyes. Her blond hair was plaited and twisted like a pretzel at the back of her head. She wore a men's striped shirt with the sleeves rolled up, and overalls covered in grease stains. He looked down and noticed the heavy boots she wore.

"Hey! I know you! You were driving that thing!"

Her hand reached up and slapped over his mouth. "I. Said. Be. Quiet!" she hissed, looking anxiously over her shoulder at the door. "Do you want to save yourself and your brothers?"

He nodded. Her hand never left his mouth.

"Do you want to hang for murder?"

He shook his head.

"Then do exactly as I say."

# CHAPTER 7

"I know you're in here."

Otto's voice echoed through the dark garage, above the din of the steam carriage boiler. "The door was locked. If you think you can steal that steam carriage and get away, you're quite mistaken."

He lifted a lantern, scanning the garage. He couldn't see them. Night had fallen, and the gaslights of the main street were too far away to be of any use. The garage held deep shadows even the lantern couldn't pierce, at least not from the doorway. He took two steps forward, sliding the door shut behind him.

"Only two people held keys to the cabinet. I doubt you've the brains to know how to start the boiler on the steam carriage. So I suspect my worthless niece is also in here. Mathilde, come out this instant." He swung the lantern in a wide arc, but it still revealed only indistinct shapes and rusted machinery. "I cannot believe what an ungrateful wretch you are! After I took you in and raised you as my own child, to betray me for a stranger? It's unforgivable."

"You and I have different ideas of what behavior is unforgivable, Uncle." Her voice echoed through the garage. The sound bounced off the pieces of metal that hung all around. It sounded as though she was near the back, but it was difficult to tell exactly where.

"Where is the Hamm boy? I will kill him either way, but helping me might keep you out of the workhouse," he sneered.

"The Hamm boy is over here, you cowardly old blowhard," Elias called out from the darkest corner of the garage. They had to maneuver him into just the right spot.

"Brave boy. It's a pity you and your brothers couldn't see sense. It looks like I'm going to have to shoot you here, after all. You think you've helped yourselves by starting the steam carriage to confuse me, but the noise will cover the sound of gunfire nicely."

Otto stepped into the glow of the open furnace, brandishing the pistol. He raised the lantern to see into the corner where he heard Elias' voice.

Suddenly an earsplitting screech startled him.

A low-pitched roar filled the space, vibrating the tools and mechanical parts that hung from every rafter and beam.

Otto whirled towards the steam carriage. The

fans spun wildly. Wind whipped the tail of his coat like tall grass in a Kansas gale. His beaver hat flew from his head, straight into the furnace.

The blazing coal furnace was right behind him, doors thrown wide. He could feel its heat, along with the swirling maelstrom building only feet away. The metal parts and tools hanging everywhere swung faster, clashing against each other. The rust and dust from the floor swirled, clouding everything in a red haze.

His polished boots began to slide backward across the dusty floor of the garage. He waved his arms madly, like a goose attempting to take flight off a lake. The wind lifted him. The toes of his boots scraped for purchase on boards worn smooth as kid leather.

Blistering heat from the furnace met violent air, spinning him like the wheel on an overturned wagon. He cried out, but it was impossible to hear over the cacophony of howling wind and rattling metal. The winds wrapped around him and he spiraled, screaming and flailing, into the furnace.

From the other side of the garage, Mattie dragged herself hand over hand against the wind back to the W.O.L.F.E. The nascent twister had flung her across the room. She'd only barely missed being skewered on a metal hook hung from the wall. Her braid had pulled free of its pins. It whipped in the wind like a rattlesnake striking. She finally managed to grab the kill switch and slammed it down.

The wind died instantly.

Elias dropped his arms, which had been wrapped around his head, and pried himself off the wall where he'd been pinned. He and Mattie staggered to the furnace. Her voice came out in ragged puffs.

"It seems . . . my uncle . . . has died . . . in a tragic . . . accident, *ja*?" She coughed up what seemed like a gallon of dust. Elias steadied her as she nearly fell over. Her eyes were red and streaming with tears. Whether it was from the dirt in her eyes, the relief of being free from her uncle, or the pain of losing her last living relative, she couldn't say for certain. It was probably all those things and more. The young farmer patted her back, coughing and hacking his own lungs clear.

"Terrible shame," he rasped, his throat still clogged with metal dust. "Too bad neither of us could reach him in time."

# EPILOGUE

William was looking better every day. Elias suspected not hearing his brothers squabble constantly might have hastened his recovery. They'd finally settled their differences, he and Jeremiah. Although Elias never would like living in a soddy.

It was the middle of spring, and Elias was in the field with Job, the new farm hand. He was green as an onion sprout, but a quick learner. His father was a friend of their Pa's. The boy was determined to go out West. With five older brothers, his prospects were poor back home. The kid was already sweet on the daughter of the town's mercantile owner.

A letter from Mattie had just arrived the day before. He had it folded and tucked into his coat pocket. She said things were going fine out in San Francisco. She had been able to sell her devices at a good price as soon as she arrived in town. It seemed several folk shared her mistrust of machines powered by alchemy. They were happy to buy her simpler clockworks instead.

As promised, she'd disassembled the W.O.L.F.E. after arriving safely in the city in the steam carriage. She'd built other machines from its parts, none of which would blow a man's house down. Now she had rented some space in a warehouse. According to the letter, she was doing a brisk business as a tinker under the name Matthias.

Elias had a hard time imagining anyone would believe she was a young man, but she was determined to continue the ruse. Her time with her uncle had left her deeply mistrustful of others. If she felt safer posing as a boy, he supposed they'd both done worse things. Even now, he regretted the death of her uncle. He had been a madman, and would have killed them both and his brothers besides, but they both still wished they could have found another way to stop him. He hadn't told Jeremiah or William the whole story of what had happened in the railroad garage. He doubted he ever would.

Soon, William would be ready to start working on the farm again. He and Jeremiah had agreed. Once Will was back on his feet, Elias would leave the farm. He planned to visit Mattie in San Francisco first. She promised to help him pick up odd jobs as a handyman or delivery boy, until he could find a steam ship willing to take him on as crew. According to Mattie, ships passed through San Francisco heading to and from every port in the world, from the far east to South America to Africa.

It was hard, dangerous work. He'd probably never get rich at it, but he didn't care. He was used to hard work, and he didn't figure anything would ever be much more dangerous than setting off a twister inside a garage full of sharp objects.

He was going to see the world, with his brothers' blessing. He thought of the pile of books Will had carried out from Philadelphia, and how disappointing his own life's story had seemed in comparison just a few months ago. When he came back to visit his brothers, he'd have plenty of exciting tales to share.

He couldn't imagine a better ending than that.

# AUTHOR'S NOTE

It may seem silly to talk about historical accuracy in a story where people create tornados with a steam engine, but I wanted to let you know a few interesting bits of research I found in writing this tale. We're all familiar with the eclectic building materials the Three Little Pigs used in the original fairy tale.

Did you know that pioneers in the Great Plains really did build with straw? In fact, there's a straw bale church built in 1928 that's still stands in Nebraska. Unfortunately, one of the earliest straw bale buildings was a schoolhouse reported as being eaten by cows only a few years after it was built. The owners hadn't covered it with adobe!

I was a little uncertain about the wattle-and-daub "house made of sticks" in North America. However, I discovered that like Europeans, Native Americans used this building technique. There's a wattle-and-daub house in Etowah State Park in Georgia. It was constructed by native craftsmen and volunteers, and completed in 2008.

As for bricks, real ones would have been incredibly difficult to come by on the Kansas prairie, but bricks made of sod were extremely common. Like the straw bale church, some of these structures still stand today. So Jeremiah (and the oldest little pig from the fairy tale) probably had a decent point in their choice of building material.

I hope you've enjoyed *Blowhard*. Set in the 1870s, it is chronologically the first book in **The Clockwork Republics**, my series of steampunk retellings of classic fairy tales.

If you're you'd like to hear more about my writing, please visit my website at www.katinafrench.com.

# ABOUT THE AUTHOR

Katina French is a science fiction and fantasy author from southern Indiana. An award-winning copywriter, she's been writing professionally for over 20 years. Recent works include "The Clockwork Republics Series," a set of steampunk retellings of classic fairy tales, as well as the space adventure serial BELLE STARR.

Ms. French writes fast-paced, humor-laced adventure stories with a touch of mystery and romance that appeal to young adults and the young at heart.

CPSIA information can be obtained at www.ICGtesting.com
Printed in the USA
LVOW01s0225100415

433933LV00015B/150/P

9 781940 938080